Pete the Cat
Talent Show Trouble

by Kimberly & James Dean

HARPER

An Imprint of HarperCollinsPublishers

ISBN 978-0-06-297416-7

21 22 23 24 25   CWM   10 9 8 7 6 5 4 3 2 1

First Edition

Pete is excited. His town is having a talent show! Pete loves shows. He loves performing for the crowd and making people happy.

Pete can't wait to sign up.
He knows just what he wants to do.
He will play his guitar!

Callie is going to dance.

Alligator is doing magic.

Gus is playing his drums.

Pete sees a familiar name at the bottom of the sign-up list. It's Grumpy Toad's!

TALENT SHOW
SIGN UP

NAME	TALENT
Callie	Dance
Alligator	Magic
Gus	Drums
Grumpy Toad	Guitar

Grumpy Toad is playing his guitar, just like Pete.
Pete is worried. Grumpy Toad is his best friend.
How can they compete against each other?

On his way home, Pete hears music coming from Grumpy Toad's house. Grumpy Toad is practicing his guitar.

"Your song sounds super groovy," Pete says. "Is that what you're playing in the talent show?"

"Yup," says Grumpy Toad. "I've been working on it all week!"

"Neat," says Pete. "I'm playing guitar in the talent show, too!
I hope I can be as good as you."

Pete goes to his house.
He takes out his guitar.
"What song should I play?" he asks himself.

Pete starts to play.
Suddenly, Grumpy Toad's music gets very loud.
Pete cannot hear himself play!

Pete does not worry.
He puts on headphones.
   Now Grumpy Toad can play
as loud as he wants, and Pete
can still hear his guitar.

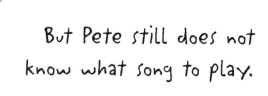

But Pete still does not
know what song to play.

Pete decides to write a new song.
He will show the judges that he has *two* talents.
Pete tries out some notes.

They sound great, but he can't
come up with the right words.

Just then, Pete sees Grumpy Toad listening through his window.

When Grumpy Toad sees Pete looking at him, he runs back to his house.

Pete takes off his headphones.
He goes to Grumpy Toad's house.

Grumpy Toad is trying to write a new song, too!

FRIENDS ARE GROOVY

MEOW

MEOW

MUSIC ROCKS

GROOVY CAT

PRACTICE MAKES PURR-FECT

EVERYONE HAS TALENT

HARPER
An Imprint of HarperCollinsPublishers   www.harpercollinschildrens.com   Illustrations © 2021 by James Dean

Pete listens to Grumpy Toad's song.
The lyrics are nifty.

Pete pokes his head
into Grumpy Toad's room.
"Your song is super
cool," he says. "Keep up
the good work!"

"Pete," Grumpy Toad says. "You aren't supposed to be listening to me. We are competing against each other."

Pete shrugs. "I like listening to you play.
Your songs are so good."

Grumpy Toad smiles. "Thanks, Pete. I like listening
to you play, too. I don't understand. Don't you
want to win? Shouldn't you be practicing?"

"Winning would be super neat," Pete says, "but it is not everything. I just want to have fun."

"Fun?" Grumpy Toad asks.
"Yeah, fun!" Pete says. "The room will be full of cool cats. I just want my music to make them happy. That's what music is all about."

"You're right," he tells Pete. "I got so caught up in the idea of winning, I forgot why I even *play* guitar."

Grumpy Toad smiles at Pete. "Thanks for reminding me."

Just then, Pete has a cool idea.

"I wrote a new tune. And you wrote new words.
What if we combine our songs? If we work together,
our song will be the hippest thing ever!"
"Yes!" Grumpy Toad shouts. "And we can be a team."

Pete and Grumpy Toad get right to work.
They put Grumpy Toad's words and Pete's tune together.

Grumpy Toad and Pete practice playing their song together.

They practice singing their song together.

Pete was right. The song is super neat!

Finally, the big day comes.

Callie does ballet.

Alligator pulls a
rabbit from a hat.

Gus plays a drum solo.

Grumpy Toad and Pete are next.
They rock out on their guitars.

The crowd loves their new song!

It is time to announce the winners.
Callie gets first place.
Grumpy Toad and Pete come in second.

"Sorry we didn't win, Grumpy Toad," Pete says.
Grumpy Toad smiles. "That's okay. We had fun.
And we did it together!"
Pete agrees. Having his best friend by his side
feels pretty neat!